Amazing World of the
DINOSAURS

Written by Sarah Albee
Reviewed by Robert E. Budliger

SilverDolphin

Silver Dolphin Books
An imprint of Printers Row Publishing Group
A division of Readerlink Distribution Services, LLC
10350 Barnes Canyon Road, Suite 100, San Diego, CA 92121
www.silverdolphinbooks.com

Copyright © 2017 Silver Dolphin Books

All notations of errors or omissions should be addressed to
Silver Dolphin Books, Editorial Department, at the above address.

A component of ISBN 978-1-68412-604-0. Not for individual sale.

Manufactured, printed, and assembled in Shenzhen, China.
First printing, August 2018. HH/08/18

22 21 20 19 18   1 2 3 4 5

ART AND PHOTOGRAPHY CREDITS

(t = top, b = bottom, l = left, r = right, c = center)

Front Cover: ©Silver Dolphin Books; **Title Page:** *Luis Rey/Wildlife Art Ltd.;*
Pages 4–5: ©Silver Dolphin Books 5c; *Simone End 5tr;* **Pages 6–7:** *James McKinnon 6tl, 6tlc, 6lc, 6bc;*
Peter Schouten 6rc; James McKinnon 6-7tc, 6-7bc; Peter Schouten 7tl; James McKinnon 7c, 7tc;
Luis Rey/Wildlife Art Ltd. 7tr; David Kirshner 7rc; Luis Rey/Wildlife Art Ltd. 7br; James McKinnon 7bc;
Pages 8–9: *James McKinnon;* **Pages 10–11:** *Peter Schouten 10bl; James McKinnon 10-11;*
Pages 12–13: *Luis Rey/Wildlife Art Ltd. 12-13;* ©Silver Dolphin Books 13br;
Pages 14–15: *Luis Rey/Wildlife Art Ltd. 4bl;* ©Silver Dolphin Books 14-15c;
Pages 16–17: *David Kirshner;* **Pages 18–19:** ©Silver Dolphin Books 18-19; *David Kirshner 19tr;*
Pages 20–21: *Peter Scott/Wildlife Art Ltd.;* **Pages 22–23:** *James McKinnon 22-23;* ©Silver Dolphin Books 23tr;
Pages 24–25: ©Silver Dolphin Books; **Pages 26–27:** *Kevin Stead;* **Pages 28–29:** *Peter Scott/Wildlife Art Ltd.;*
Pages 30–31: *Peter Scott/Wildlife Art Ltd. 30bl; Kevin Stead 30r; Lee Gibbons/Wildlife Art Ltd. 30-31;*
Pages 32–33: *David McAllister 32-33b; Frank Knight 33t;* **Pages 34–35:** *Simone End 34b;*
Peter Scott/Wildlife Art Ltd. 35; **Page 37:** *Peter Scott/Wildlife Art Ltd.*

Illustrations italicized above ©1999 Weldon Owen, Inc.

Diorama Imagery: ©Anderl, ©artis777, ©DM7, ©Kostyantyn Ivanyshen/Shutterstock.com

Stickers: ©artis777, ©Linda Bucklin, ©leonello calvetti, ©DM7, ©Ralf Juergen Kraft,
©Paul B. Moore, ©Bob Orsillo, ©Bombaert Patrick, ©Michael Rosskothen,
©Kostyantyn Salanda, ©Sofia Santos/Shutterstock.com

3-D model art: Robin Carter/Wildlife Art

Contents

Studying Dinosaurs

Dinosaurs were ancient reptiles that lived on earth for about 165 million years. But about 65 million years ago, all the dinosaurs died off. Today, all we have left of them are some **fossils** of bones, footprints, and other bits and pieces.

When most people think about dinosaurs, they imagine huge, ferocious creatures. But not all dinosaurs were huge. And not all of them were scary. Some types of dinosaurs had beaks, some had feathers, and others had horns. Some lived alone, and some lived in herds of a thousand or more. In fact, one of the most amazing things about these animals is how very different they were from one another. So far, scientists called **paleontologists** have discovered and named more than 700 different types of dinosaurs— but new types are still being found today.

When and Where

The history of the earth is divided into eras, and the eras are then divided into periods of time. The **Mesozoic** era— known as the Age of Dinosaurs—is divided into three periods: the **Triassic**, the **Jurassic**, and the **Cretaceous**. Today we live in the Quaternary period of the Cenozoic era. Humans have been on earth for about 4 million years. Compare that to the dinosaurs' 165 million years!

What's in a Name?

Although the word *dinosaur* means "terrible lizard," dinosaurs were not lizards! Like lizards and other modern reptiles (alligators, crocodiles, turtles), dinosaurs laid eggs. But unlike modern reptiles, dinosaurs walked with their legs directly under their bodies, not splayed out at their sides.

What's that Word?

As you read, you will see words that are in **bold**. Look for them in the glossary on pages 36–37 to learn what they mean.

The Age of Dinosaurs

TRIASSIC PERIOD

JURASSIC PERIOD

Kannemeyeria

Dinosaur diet key

- Meat-eater
- Plant-eater

Scaphognathus, pterosaur

Eoraptor

Plateosaurus

Dilophosaurus

Allosaurus

PREHISTORIC TIMES

PALEOZOIC ERA

550 million years ago

CRETACEOUS PERIOD

Stegosaurus

Euoplocephalus

Deinonychus

Mamenchisaurus

Barosaurus

Lambeosaurus

Tyrannosaurus rex

Triceratops

TRIASSIC	JURASSIC	CRETACEOUS	
MESOZOIC ERA			CENOZOIC ERA
248 million years ago	206 million years ago	144 million years ago	65 million years ago	Today

Life in the Triassic

When dinosaurs first appeared, the earth was one enormous landmass surrounded by water. Dense forests—filled with ferns, palmlike plants, and cone-bearing trees—grew near the coastlines. There were no flowers anywhere, and most of the land was a hot, dry desert.

Nearly all of the animals lived near the coast, where it was easier to find food and water. Reptiles and huge fish hunted in the ocean. More reptiles—ancestors of the earliest dinosaurs—hunted on land. Spiders, scorpions, centipedes, and insects scuttled among the plants and desert sands. Many other kinds of animals had evolved and disappeared by the time the Triassic came to an end. But not the dinosaurs. They survived and thrived, with new **species** eventually spreading all over the earth.

Look Out Below!

The first dinosaurs shared the earth with the first crocodiles, tortoises, and rat-size mammals. Up in the air swooped flying reptiles, known as **pterosaurs**. Pterosaurs such as *Pterodactylus* and *Pteranodon* were relatives of dinosaurs.

During the late Triassic, a Plateosaurus *might have grazed on some ferns alongside meat-eating* Coelophysis. *The meat-eaters were probably more interested in eating small lizards than in attacking the huge plant-eater.*

Jurassic Giants

Some of the biggest animals ever to walk on land appeared during the Jurassic period. The **sauropods** were among these. These **herbivores** had thick feet and legs, similar to those of a present-day elephant. They had long necks that allowed them to browse in the treetops, or to sweep their heads from side to side to graze on ground plants. Their peglike teeth ripped off leaves, which were then digested in an organ called the gizzard. Their huge size helped them scare off most **predators**. Some sauropods probably fought off enemies by cracking their whiplike tails. They may also have traveled in herds.

By the Jurassic, many meat-eating dinosaurs had evolved into even larger animals. *Allosaurus* was one of the biggest **carnivores**, standing as tall as an elephant. Like modern wolves, *Allosaurus* probably hunted in packs and went after large **prey**.

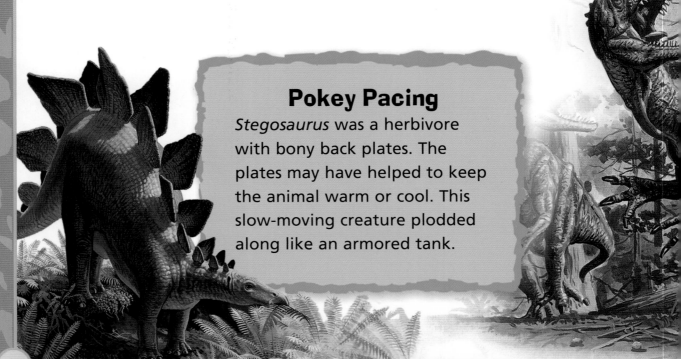

Pokey Pacing

Stegosaurus was a herbivore with bony back plates. The plates may have helped to keep the animal warm or cool. This slow-moving creature plodded along like an armored tank.

A mother Barosaurus *rises to her full height* to protect her baby from attack by an Allosaurus, *a fierce Jurassic carnivore.*

Cretaceous Creatures

Over a long period of time, many types of dinosaurs, such as *Allosaurus* and *Stegosaurus*, gradually disappeared. But during the Cretaceous period other kinds of dinosaurs developed to take their place.

One of these groups was the **tyrannosaurids**. The best known of this group, *Tyrannosaurus rex*, ruled what we now think of as the North American continent in the late Cretaceous. This carnivore walked on two legs and grew to be 40 feet long. Its terrifying jaws flashed about 60 sharp teeth.

Plenty of smaller but equally fierce carnivores thrived during this time, too. These creatures had large brains for their small size. Many of them hunted in packs.

Many herbivorous dinosaurs adapted special features for defense. The heavy bone at the end of the Ankylosaurus' tail formed a club that could do serious damage, even to an attacking Tyrannosaurus.

Triceratops

Triceratops probably used its facial horns to defend itself against attackers. But it probably also locked horns with other *Triceratops* over territory or would-be mates.

Dinosaur Mysteries

Dinosaurs have been **extinct** for 65 million years. And everything we know about them comes from the study of their fossilized bones, footprints, and some smaller bits. Considering this, it's truly amazing that we know as much as we do about these remarkable animals. But it is not at all surprising that so many mysteries remain.

One mystery is if dinosaurs were **warm-blooded** like modern birds or **cold-blooded** like modern reptiles. Why would it matter? Warm-blooded animals need more food, and they grow quickly. If a huge dinosaur, such as *Brachiosaurus*, were warm-blooded, it would have needed to eat tons of **vegetation** every day—and its young would have taken about ten years to grow to full size. If it were cold-blooded, it would have needed much less food, but its young might have taken 100 years to grow to adulthood!

Camouflage or Color?

We don't know what colors dinosaurs were, but we can take a guess by looking at animals today. *Edmontosaurus* (top) **migrated** across open plains, so it probably had a coloring that matched its surroundings. *Coelophysis* (bottom) was a tigerlike creature, so it may have had stripes that helped it hide from predators.

Pumping Blood

How did a huge, long-necked **sauropod** such as *Barosaurus* circulate blood throughout its enormous body? How was its heart able to pump blood up its 30-foot neck and into its brain? Some paleontologists estimate that its heart would have had to weigh over 1½ tons to manage that task. Others think that it must have had more than one heart. Since soft tissues like hearts don't fossilize, it's doubtful that we will ever know.

Biggest and Longest!

The biggest of all the dinosaurs were the herbivorous sauropods. Sauropods had thick feet and legs (like an elephant) and very long necks, which were balanced by their long tails.

Although the sauropods' skeletons were huge, they were light. Pockets of air in the neck bones of these dinosaurs made their necks extremely light and allowed the animals to hold their heads upright and move them around easily.

Because sauropods were so large and because they traveled in herds, many carnivorous dinosaurs simply stayed away from them.

Most carnivorous dinosaurs were not huge. The biggest discovered so far is *Giganotosaurus*. This dinosaur had lightweight leg bones, which allowed it to chase—and catch—fast-moving prey.

Stretching Necks

Mamenchisaurus (near right), *Diplodocus* (center), and *Brachiosaurus* (far right) were among the biggest and heaviest animals that ever lived. They all had incredibly long necks with relatively tiny heads on top. A modern giraffe's neck looks short in comparison!

Heavy Duty!

Brachiosaurus was one of the largest and heaviest sauropods. But compared to other sauropods, it had a relatively short tail, which kept it from being ranked among the longest. By some estimates *Brachiosaurus* weighed up to 50 tons—as much as 10 bull elephants. It swallowed huge stones (called **gastroliths**) on purpose. These stones ground up the vegetation inside the animal's gut and allowed for digestion.

Brainy Business

Most of the small dinosaurs were carnivores, and they seemed to have big brains for their size. They also had relatively long legs and arms. How did they manage to survive living side by side with their much bigger carnivore and herbivore cousins? Paleontologists believe they made their homes in thick undergrowth or around craggy, rocky places where larger animals couldn't fit.

One of the smallest carnivores was *Compsognathus*, which was about 3 feet long. It had a narrow, pointed head, a flexible neck, and a tail that was long for its body size. It probably ate large insects, lizards, and small **mammals**—it may even have swallowed them whole.

On the other hand, *Stegosaurus* had the smallest brain relative to its size. It was 25 feet long and had a brain the size of a walnut!

A Head Case

Troodon (top) had the largest brain relative to the size of its body. This sharp-eyed, birdlike **theropod** was probably a deadly hunter. *Tyrannosaurus* (bottom) had one of the largest heads, but its brain was relatively small. A human brain takes up most of the head and allows us the ability for complex thought.

Dino Speedsters

For many of the smaller dinosaurs, the best defense against predators was to run away. The speedier ones were usually able to outrun predators.

But many large dinosaurs had speed on their side as well. The speediest carnivores had small bodies and long back legs.

The fastest group of dinosaurs was probably the **ornithomimids**. These were carnivores that probably fed on small mammals, insects, and lizards (the group may also have included herbivores), and they stood about as tall as a human, although some were even bigger!

The ornithomimids resembled modern ostriches and may have reached speeds as fast as 40 miles per hour (mph), allowing them to outrun larger predators.

In the Fast Lane

Ornithomimids ran faster than a human but not as fast as an ostrich.

| Fastest human 22.8 mph | *Dromiceiomimus* 30 mph | *Struthiomimus* 40 mph | Ostrich 50 mph |

Gallimimus, *the biggest ornithomimid, ran so quickly and changed direction so suddenly that it could easily avoid the scary but slow-moving* Albertosaurus.

Good Defense!

Speed was no defense for slow-moving herbivores, but they had other ways of putting off predators. Size, for example. Some dinosaurs were so huge, no predator would even think of attacking them. Others defended themselves with horns, clublike tails, or skin as thick as armor.

Triceratops had bony frills and horns protecting its neck.

Boneheads!

A group of dinosaurs called **pachycephalosaurs** lived during the Cretaceous period. These dinosaurs had very thick skulls. Some had flat heads, while others had large, domed heads. Some paleontologists think these dinosaurs used their heads as battering rams, although new evidence indicates that the headgear may have been only ornamental—a show-off way to attract mates.

Tough Guys

The large carnivorous theropods were the terrors of their Mesozoic world.

Tyrannosaurus rex, which means "king of the tyrant lizards," was among the largest and fiercest of the dinosaurs. Its huge mouth held about 60 teeth, and each one was the size of a carving knife.

Before *Tyrannosaurus*, there was *Allosaurus*, which weighed almost 4 tons and was about the length of three cars. It stood as tall as an elephant. After *Tyrannosaurus*, there was *Giganotosaurus*. These three were among the biggest of the tough guys.

But plenty of smaller carnivores could be just as vicious, especially when they hunted in packs. *Velociraptor* and *Dromaeosaurus* were equipped with sharp teeth and deadly claws. *Ornitholestes* was probably no bigger than a human, but it weighed only as much as a medium-sized dog. Its prey included large insects, lizards, young dinosaurs, and small mammals. It may have grabbed its victims in its sharp claws and swallowed them alive!

Claws Count!

Utahraptor was less than half the size of *Tyrannosaurus*, but its fingers and toes had sharp claws. Each hind foot also had an extra-large claw with a razor-sharp tip that never touched the ground. These "meat hooks" were more than 12 inches long.

High in the Sky

Up in the Mesozoic sky flew many different kinds of creatures such as flying and gliding reptiles and—somewhat later in the era—early birds.

Although some may have looked like flying dinosaurs, the pterosaurs were only distant relatives since feathered dinosaurs most likely did not fly; unlike the pterosaurs, their feathers were probably used to keep their bodies warm.

Some of the pterosaurs were as small as sparrows, while others were as big as a small airplane! How could such huge bodies stay airborne? Their bones were long, light, and hollow, and probably held pockets of air to make them even lighter.

Some paleontologists believe that pterosaurs clomped around on all fours and thus could not move well on land. But they may have been able to climb trees by digging into the bark with the claws on their wings.

The largest pterosaurs most likely did not fly, but rather hitched rides on air currents and glided along on their enormous wings.

Birdosaur?

The theory that modern birds descended from certain theropod dinosaurs (and not from flying pterosaurs) has been gaining popularity. Pterosaurs may have looked birdlike, but they did not survive the Cretaceous extinction. Certain two-footed theropods, on the other hand, probably looked a lot more like weird birds than like giant lizards.

Baby Talk

Like all birds and most reptiles, dinosaurs laid eggs. At one time paleontologists believed that all dinosaur mothers laid their eggs and then went on their way, without staying around to care for their young—much the way modern turtles and lizards do. But recent discoveries have changed that **theory**.

While some dinosaur babies did not need help and were able to move about as soon as they hatched, others depended on their parents for survival. Fossil discoveries show that some dinosaur parents built nests for their eggs and stayed nearby to feed and care for their young. But for how long? We just don't know.

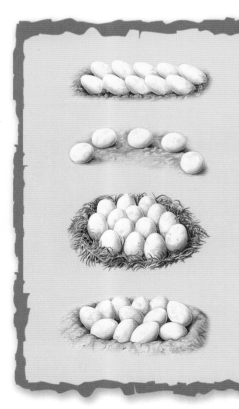

Nursery Style

Dinosaur mothers laid their eggs in different ways. Some laid pairs of eggs in tidy lines. Others laid their eggs in an arc along the ground. Others lined the nest with leaves and plants to keep the eggs warm. Certain dinosaur mothers built their nests close together, probably for protection from predators.

Touchdown!

The biggest dinosaur egg discovered so far was about the size of a football. But considering how enormous some types of dinosaurs grew to be, dinosaur eggs were surprisingly small.

The Dinosaurs Disappear

This much we know: About 65 million years ago a giant space rock—a comet or an asteroid—slammed into the earth with incredible force. The rock was so huge and landed with such force that it left a crater more than 100 miles wide in what is now the Yucatan Peninsula of Mexico.

Many scientists believe that the impact created firestorms that filled the air with soot and smoke for many years, causing the eventual disappearance of many plants and animals, including dinosaurs. This massive die-off of so many living things is known as the **Cretaceous extinction**. It is the most widely held theory to explain the disappearance of dinosaurs. But there are other theories, too: continuous volcanic eruptions and rapid climate changes. We will probably never know the exact cause with certainty.

Just Dumb Luck?

Paleontologists believe that by the end of the Cretaceous extinction, as many as half of all the animal species on earth had died out. What puzzles these scientists is why some animals survived. Why did the dinosaurs and flying reptiles die off, while crocodiles, turtles, lizards, birds, and ancient mammals survived?

Other Extinction Theories

The world's climate became too cold, and dinosaurs froze or starved to death.

The world's climate became too hot for dinosaurs to survive.

Volcanic eruptions poisoned the air and the land.

Fossil Clues

Everything we know about dinosaurs has been carefully chipped out of rocks and dirt all around the world by paleontologists. But there is still so much we don't know. New discoveries about dinosaurs are being made all the time but very few dinosaurs left fossil remains.

The conditions had to be just right for an ancient animal to leave any evidence of its existence. It had to die in a place where its body would be quickly covered by sand, mud, or water. When that happened, usually only the hard parts of the animal (bones and teeth) became fossilized. But sometimes the soft parts of an ancient animal (skin, scales, feathers, even droppings) left imprints in the surrounding rock. These softer parts hint at what these ancient animals looked like, what they ate, and how they moved. By studying their fossilized nests and eggs, we can even learn something about how dinosaurs took care of their babies.

Foot Finds

Fossilized footprints reveal fascinating information. Paleontologists use them to estimate a dinosaur's weight and even its speed. Footprints can also tell us about the behavior of an entire dinosaur herd. In some herds, the bigger animals moved in front and along the sides, protecting the smaller ones on the inside from predators.

How a Fossil Is Formed

1. A dinosaur body washes into a river. Soon only the bones remain.

2. The skeleton is buried under sand or mud. The bones are replaced by minerals over thousands of years, forming fossils as hard as stone.

3. Movements inside the earth bring the fossilized bones back up to the surface. **Erosion** uncovers the bones, and people discover them.

Dino Descendants

Are birds the descendants of dinosaurs? This theory is gaining acceptance by many paleontologists. Birds today don't look much like their dinosaur ancestors, but they do share many physical similarities: a wishbone, swiveling wrists, and three forward-pointing toes on each foot.

Recently paleontologists discovered that dinosaurs had a breathing system very similar to birds—and like birds, many dinosaurs had light bones. Alligators and crocodiles are also probable relatives of dinosaurs, but they are not quite so closely related.

Lucky Break

In 2003 a team of paleontologists discovered a massive *Tyrannosaurus* bone. They were forced to saw the bone in half so they could load it onto a helicopter. From the bone's core, tiny bits of brown tissue fell out. When these bits were tested, scientists learned that the animal had been dead for 68 million years and that the tissue resembled that of a chicken. This evidence further supports the theory that birds are related to dinosaurs.

The Hips Matter

Paleontologists divide all types of dinosaurs into two main groups according to the shape of the dinosaur's hip bones. The **saurischians** had hips shaped like those of a lizard (top), and the **ornithischians** had hips shaped like those of a bird (bottom). All the carnivores belonged to the lizard-hipped group, as did a few of the herbivores. All the other herbivores were bird-hipped.

Glossary

carnivore: an animal that only eats meat

cold-blooded: having a body temperature that changes with the natural surroundings; for example, snakes and lizards needing sun for heat

Cretaceous: a period of time that began about 145 million years ago and ended about 65 million years ago

Cretaceous extinction: the massive die-off of the dinosaurs at the end of the Cretaceous period

erosion: the wearing away of the surface of the earth by the action of water, wind, or glacial ice

extinct: gone forever

fossils: the remains or imprints of an ancient thing found in rocks or stony soil

herbivore: an animal that only eats plants

gastroliths: fossils of stones that sauropods swallowed to aid digestion

Jurassic: a period of time that began about 205 million years ago and ended about 145 million years ago

mammals: warm-blooded animals that have hair (at some stage of their life) and feed their young milk produced by the mother

Mesozoic: the Age of Dinosaurs era, which began about 245 million years ago and ended about 65 million years ago

migrate: to travel regularly from one place to another, often from season to season, usually to breed or search for food

ornithischians: bird-hipped dinosaurs that ate plants; one of the two orders of dinosaurs

ornithomimids: a group of herbivores and carnivores that were the fastest of the dinosaurs; resembled the modern-day ostrich

pachycephalosaurs: a group of herbivores with domed heads; referred to as the "boneheads"

paleontologists: scientists who study ancient plants and animals

predators: animals that hunt other animals for food

prey: animals that are hunted by other animals for food

pterosaurs: flying reptiles that evolved during the late Triassic period

saurischians: lizard-hipped dinosaurs, primarily carnivores but some were herbivores and some ate both meat and plants; one of the two orders of dinosaurs

sauropods: a group of giant herbivore lizard-hipped dinosaurs that existed from the late Triassic to the end of the Cretaceous; included some of the largest animals known

species: closely related animals that can produce offspring

theory: an idea that is the starting point for an investigation

theropod: a carnivore, usually with small forelimbs

Triassic: a period of time that began about 248 million years ago and ended about 205 million years ago

tyrannosaurids: a group of the largest carnivorous dinosaurs that ruled the earth during the Cretaceous

vegetation: plant life

warm-blooded: having a body temperature that stays the same when the temperature of the natural surroundings changes

3-D Model Instructions

Complete one model at a time. Press out the pieces and arrange them as shown. Using the numbers on the pictures here, match the slots and assemble your 3-D dinosaurs.

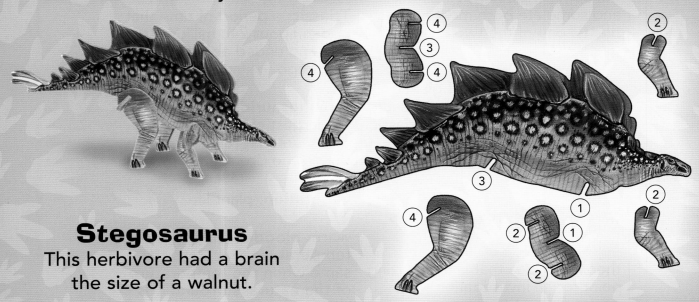

Stegosaurus

This herbivore had a brain the size of a walnut.

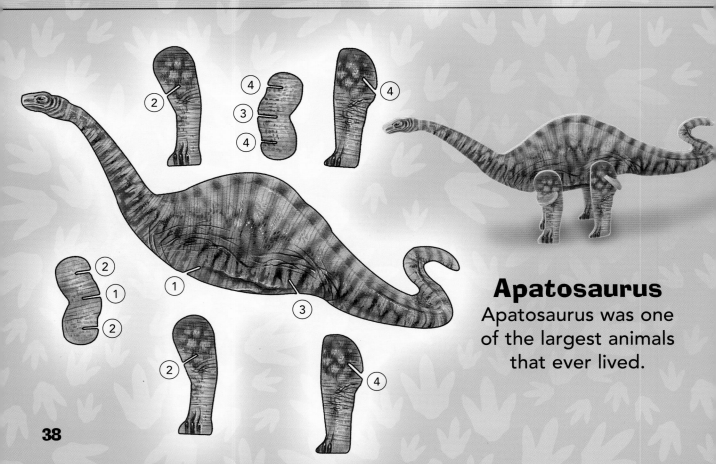

Apatosaurus

Apatosaurus was one of the largest animals that ever lived.

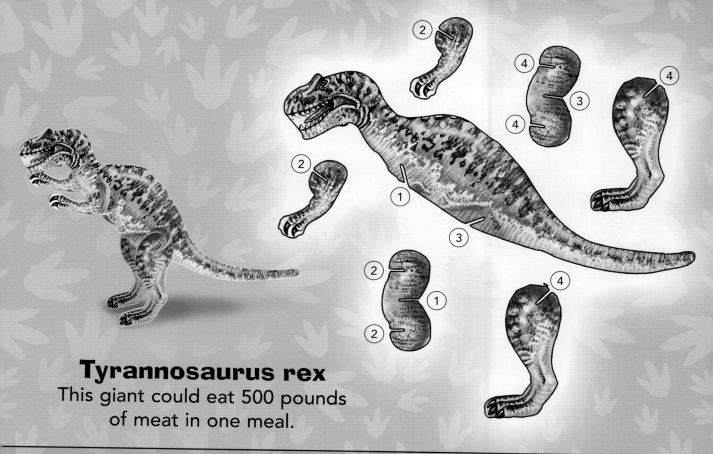

Tyrannosaurus rex
This giant could eat 500 pounds
of meat in one meal.

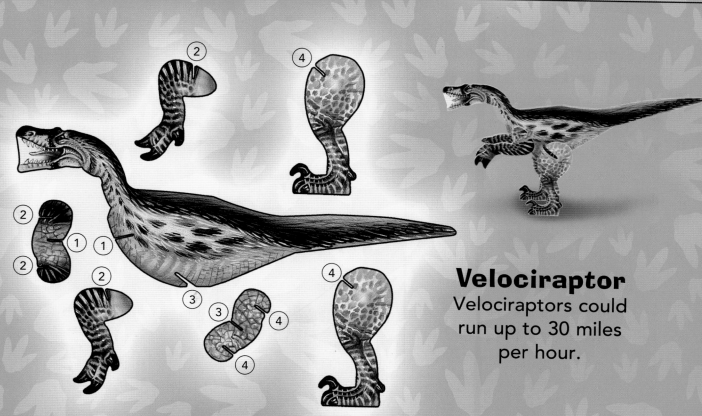

Velociraptor
Velociraptors could
run up to 30 miles
per hour.

Diorama Instructions

Bring your own world of dinosaurs to life by building a beautiful diorama. It's easy!

1. The inside of the box lid and base will be the walls of your diorama. The unfolding board will be the floor. Decorate these with reusable stickers as desired.

2. Press out the floor figures, and fold as shown. Fold, then slide the rectangular tabs through the floor slots, folding them underneath so the figures stand upright. The tabs and slots are all the same size, so you can change the position of the figures.

3. Stand the box lid and base upright and at an angle as shown. Lay the angled back edges of the floor piece on top of the box sides. You're done!

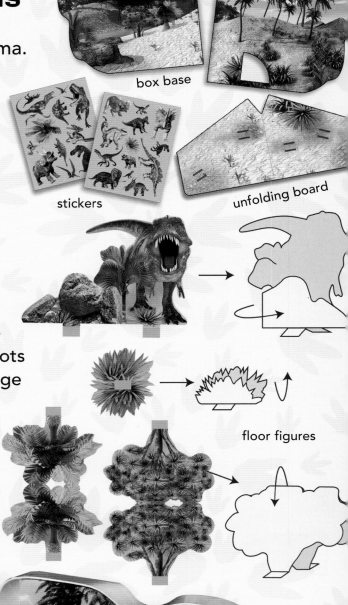

box lid

box base

stickers

unfolding board

floor figures